Golden Threads

OWLKIDS BOOKS

To all of us who have felt cracked open, scarred … embrace your golden seams, for now you are stronger,
unique, and more beautiful. And to Puppy (my son's stuffed doggie) who inspired this story — S.D.R.

For my family — M.S.

Text © 2020 Suzanne Del Rizzo
Illustrations © 2020 Miki Sato

Owlkids Books acknowledges the financial support of the Canada Council for the Arts, the Ontario Arts Council,
the Government of Canada through the Canada Book Fund (CBF) and the Government of Ontario through
the Ontario Creates Book Initiative for our publishing activities.

Published in Canada by Owlkids Books Inc., 1 Eglinton Avenue East, Toronto, ON M4P 3A1
Published in the US by Owlkids Books Inc., 1700 Fourth Street, Berkeley, CA 94710

Library and Archives Canada Cataloguing in Publication

Title: Golden threads / written by Suzanne Del Rizzo ; illustrated by Miki Sato.
Names: Del Rizzo, Suzanne, author. | Sato, Miki, 1987- illustrator.
Identifiers: Canadiana 2019014307X | ISBN 9781771473606 (hardcover)
Classification: LCC PS8607.E4825384 G64 2020 | DDC jC813/.6—dc23

Library of Congress Control Number: 2019947221

Edited by Karen Li | Designed by Diane Robertson

Manufactured in Shenzhen, Guangdong, China, in November 2020, by WKT Co. Ltd.
Job # 20CB1954

B   C   D   E   F   G

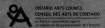

ONTARIO ARTS COUNCIL
CONSEIL DES ARTS DE L'ONTARIO
an Ontario government agency
un organisme du gouvernement de l'Ontario

Canada Council   Conseil des Arts
for the Arts   du Canada

Canada

Owl Kids
Publisher of Chirp, Chickadee and OWL
www.owlkidsbooks.com | Owlkids Books is a division of bayard canada

Golden Threads

WRITTEN BY
SUZANNE
DEL RIZZO

ILLUSTRATED BY
MIKI SATO

OWLKIDS BOOKS

Home.

High on our mountain, under our glorious ginkgo tree, happily tucked in the crook of my Emi's elbow.

It was all I'd ever known ... until the day of the storm.

"The first golden leaf!" Emi had
said, placing it inside my pocket.

Ginkgo's crown shimmered,
waving to us in the sunshine.
Behind it, gray clouds puffed.
The wind began to whistle.

At the teahouse, Obaasan greeted us
with a warm cup of kukicha twig tea.

plip ... plip ... plip ...

"More rain?" said Obaasan.

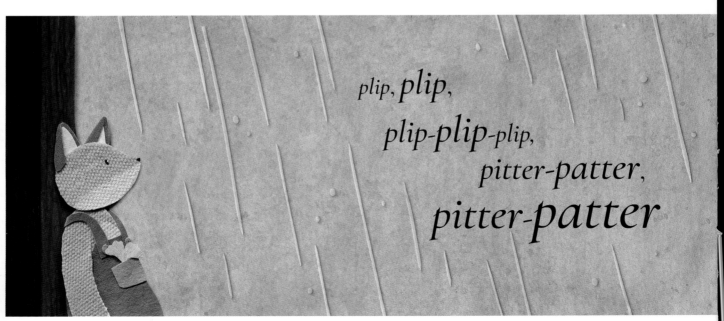

plip, plip,
plip-plip-plip,
pitter-patter,
pitter-patter

Suddenly, the rain's pattering
grew into a whirring roar ...
CRACK!

Snatched by a falling branch, I plunged head over paw.

I churned and lurched, a blur of ragged fur and froth.

And finally …
I stopped.

Day turned to night.

Like a trail of floating ginkgo leaves, the moon's reflection pointed toward home.

Finally, I was found,
but not by my Emi.

"Kiko, a friend has come to visit," the old man said, guiding a girl's hand to rest on my matted head.

Kiko washed away mud and plucked seeds nestled deep in my fur. She sniffed their sweet, woodsy scent.

"You are a long way from your pine forest," she said.

"And what treasure the fox brings!" said her ojiisan.

Kiko touched my tattered paws and
battered fur. "You must be missed."

How can I go on like THIS?
I tried to yell.

Will Emi even want me now?
But all that came out was a
tiny, frothy bubble.

"I know," Kiko whispered as she darned my fur, mending it with tiny, golden stitches.

The seasons passed ...

Whiffs of spring floated through the window, smelling of my mountainside home. "What a beautiful day!" said Kiko.

The scent of buttercups
and mountain phlox
pulled us down the path.

"Mmmmm!" said Kiko, breathing in the beauty. My stuffing puffed up, and I could feel the strength of my golden seams ...

... and we were happy.

Down the valley, autumn's frosty gusts returned. Golden speckles rippled against the shoreline.

"A golden leaf?" asked Kiko,
tracing its scalloped edge.
"From your home."

She tucked it inside my
pocket and whispered,
"I'll miss you."

Following the floating trail of
glimmering leaves, we rowed
across the lake.

In the distance, I saw my ginkgo
tree, standing tall, triumphant ...
despite one broken bough.

Hands traced my gold stitching and flicked my floppy ear. "You came home!" squealed Emi, hugging me and Kiko tight.

Kiko peeled the leaf from my pocket. "*This* showed us the way."

Beneath our golden ginkgo, we sipped warm
kukicha tea. And one by one we pieced
together the fragments of my journey.

My stitched, stuffed chest was like a seedpod
filled full to the brim.

Grateful.

Restored.

Loved.

Author's Note

This story touches on the beautiful Japanese art form of kintsugi and the ancient philosophy of wabi-sabi.

In kintsugi—translated as "golden joinery"—broken pottery is repaired with seams of gold. Traditionally, sticky resin is used to hold the broken pieces together. Once the resin dries and hardens, the seams are sanded down and painted with gold.

The kintsugi method encourages us to repair, rather than replace. Gold-filled cracks tell the story of a once-broken item and give it new value.

Kintsugi is an example of wabi-sabi. This Japanese concept has no direct translation in English. Instead, wabi-sabi is the idea of finding beauty in things that are imperfect and incomplete. It describes a way of living that accepts the natural cycle of growth and decay.

We all fall down, get hurt, feel broken ... but the stories we have to tell from our experiences make us stronger. Mending with gold teaches us that if we choose to embrace our struggles and repair ourselves with gratitude and love, we become more beautiful for having been broken.